THE
SULTAN'S
SNAKES

THE SULTAN'S SNAKES

by LORNA TURPIN

Greenwillow Books, New York

Library of Congress
Cataloging in Publication Data
Turpin, Lorna.   The sultan's snakes.
Summary: The sultan's snakes hide from him, but
the careful reader will find their hiding places
in the illustrations. [1. Snakes—Fiction.
2. Kings, queens, rulers, etc.—Fiction] I. Title.
PZ7.T882Su   [E]   80-10956   ISBN 0-688-80260-5
ISBN 0-688-84260-7 lib. bdg.

Dedicated to
LYNN and MARTIN

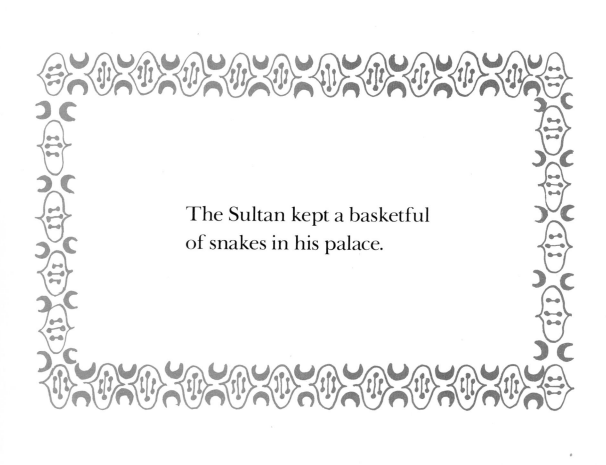

The Sultan kept a basketful
of snakes in his palace.

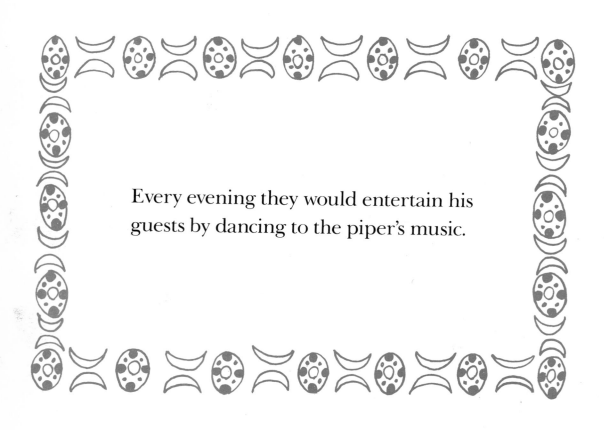

Every evening they would entertain his
guests by dancing to the piper's music.

But during the daytime, when
they were kept in the basket,
they became very bored.

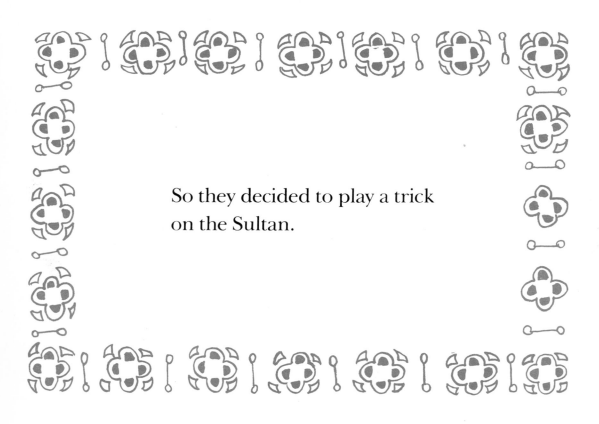

So they decided to play a trick
on the Sultan.

When he came to wish them good
morning, he found the basket empty.

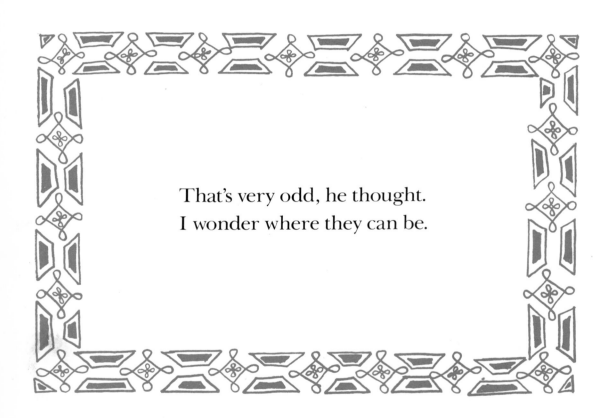

That's very odd, he thought.
I wonder where they can be.

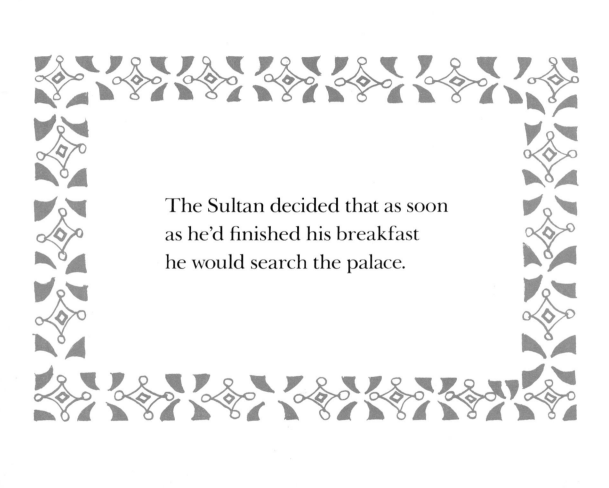

The Sultan decided that as soon
as he'd finished his breakfast
he would search the palace.

MARMALADE

First he looked in his parlor, but he couldn't see any snakes there.

So he tried the kitchen,
but still no sign.

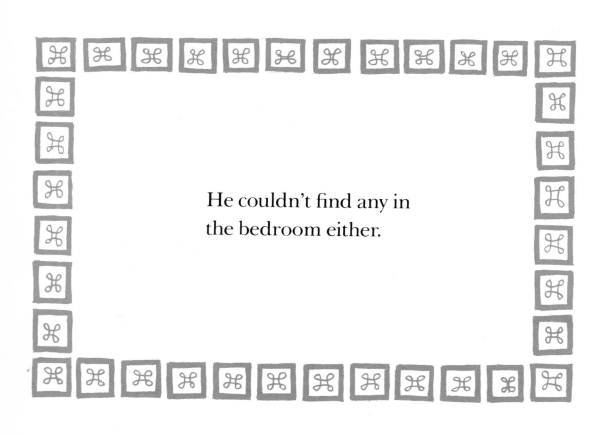

He couldn't find any in
the bedroom either.

Or the bathroom.

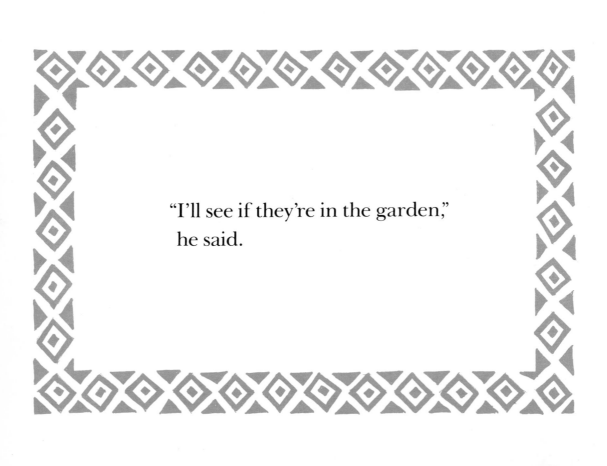

"I'll see if they're in the garden,"
he said.

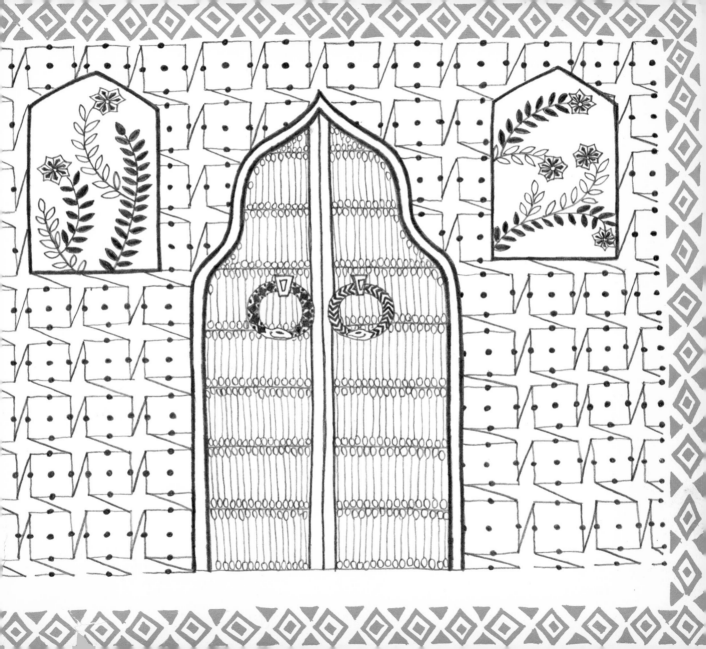

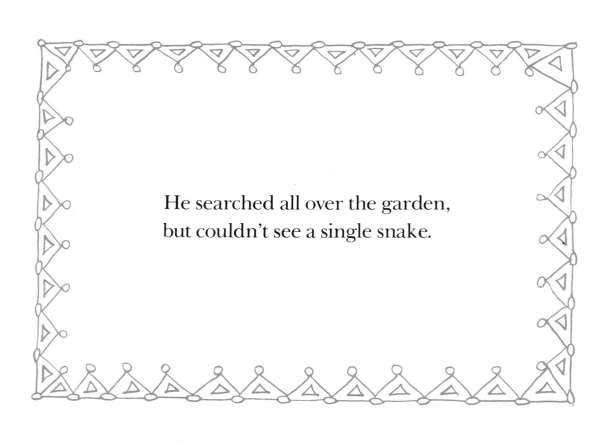

He searched all over the garden,
but couldn't see a single snake.

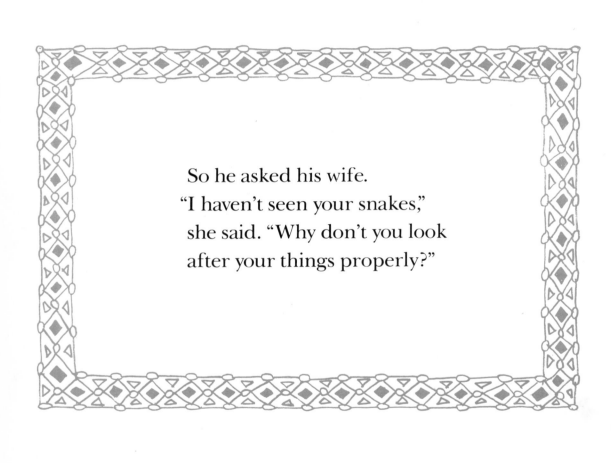

So he asked his wife.
"I haven't seen your snakes,"
she said. "Why don't you look
after your things properly?"

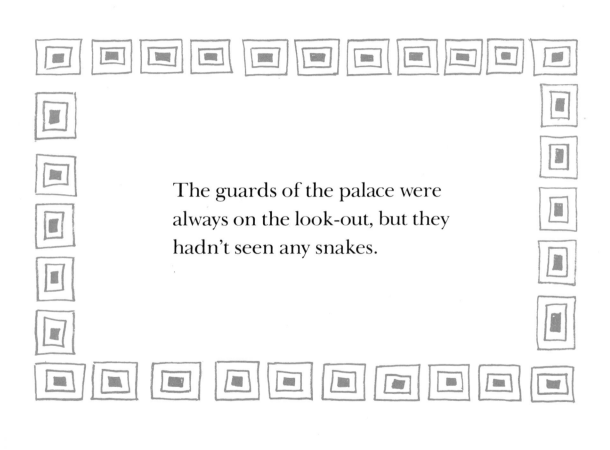

The guards of the palace were always on the look-out, but they hadn't seen any snakes.

So the Sultan asked the cleaner,
but she hadn't seen them either.

Neither had the cat.

Or the goldfish.

This is very strange, thought the Sultan. I've searched everywhere and I've asked everyone, but I still can't find them. I'll just look in the basket once more.

The snakes heard him
and hurried back.

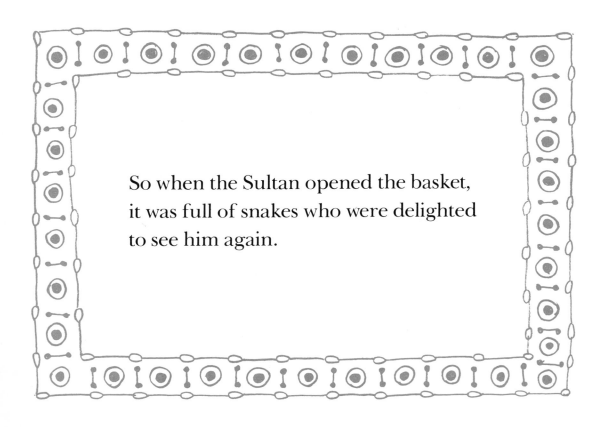

So when the Sultan opened the basket,
it was full of snakes who were delighted
to see him again.